This book belongs to:

_____

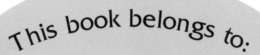

7-7-17	DATE DUE		

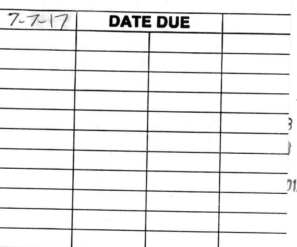

A CAMPFIRE FOR
COWBOY
BILLY

WENDY K. ULMER

illustrated by
KENNETH J. SPENGLER

rising moon

Books for Young Readers from Northland Publishing

The illustrations were done in gouache on watercolor paper
The text type was set in Friz Quadrata
The display type was set in Lithos
Composed in the United States of America
Designed and Art Directed by Rudy J. Ramos
Edited by Tom Carpenter
Production Supervised by Lisa Brownfield

Manufactured in Hong Kong by South Sea International Press Ltd.

FIRST IMPRESSION
ISBN 0-87358-681-6

Library of Congress Catalog Card Number pending

0635/15M/9-97

*For Mom and Dad, and
the Sunday night gathering
—W. K. U.*

*To my brothers, Ernie and Mike,
and to my sister, Laura, for all the great
adventures we shared growing up
—K. J. S.*

CLOMP, JINGLE, CLOMP, JINGLE, Cowboy Billy walked down the hall, his shiny boots and spurs accenting each step. Reaching high, he pushed the elevator button and waited. When the doors opened, Mr. Higgins, the elevator operator, smiled at Billy.

"Howdy, Mr. Higgins," Billy grinned.

"Where are you headed today, Pardner?"

"To the Canyon, please. I've got some mail to deliver on 44th Street."

"Looks like a pony express ride for you, Billy. Be careful!"

Outside, Billy unhitched his faithful stick horse, Splinter. The late afternoon sun painted the canyon walls with shades of red, orange, and yellow. Cloud shadows danced with the wind. Billy smiled, remembering Grandpa.

Grandpa had been Billy's best friend. Grandpa told Billy stories about cowboys and the Old West. He sent Billy a hat, chaps and vest, boots and spurs, and a turquoise Navajo ribbon shirt from Arizona. One night, when Grandpa came to visit, they climbed the fire escape to the top of the apartment building and shared the stars.

"Sure is a beautiful night," Grandpa said. "The Indians have a legend that says the stars are the campfires of those who have died and moved into the next world to dwell with the Great Spirit. Stars are the warm, twinkling campfires of special souls telling someone on earth how much they still love them."

"Do you believe that, Grandpa?"

"Of course I do," he smiled. "Home for a cowboy is anywhere he lights his campfire. Everyone has a heart full of memories, like a night full of stars.

"And our memories of love shine the brightest."

Now one of those campfires belonged to Grandpa.

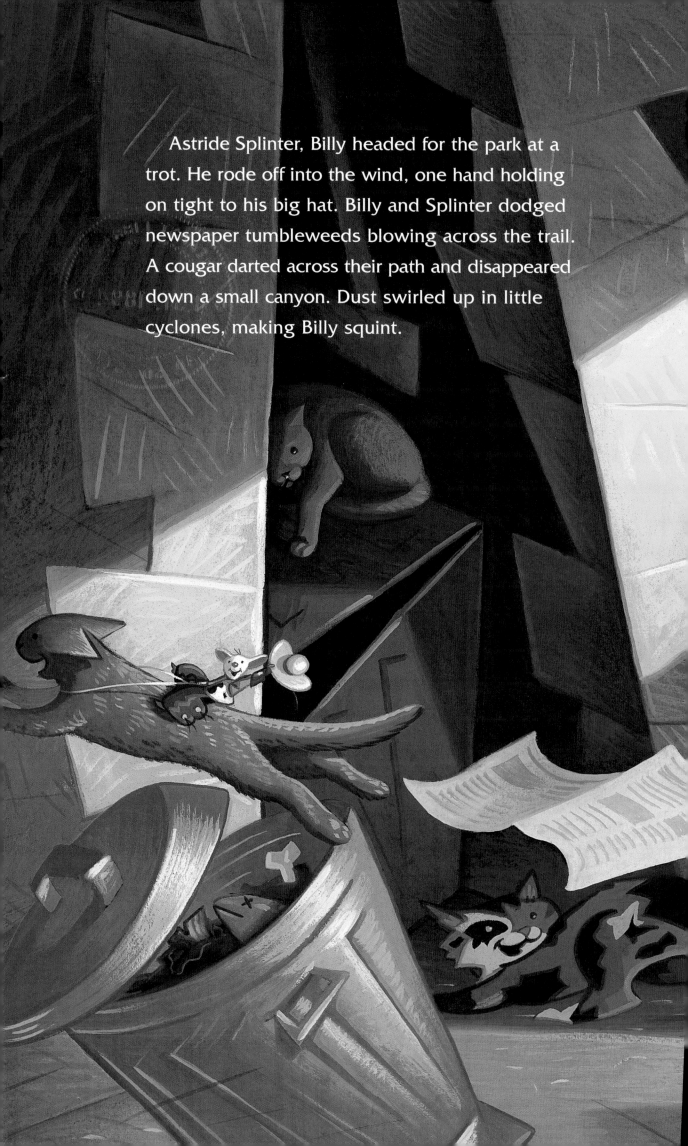

Astride Splinter, Billy headed for the park at a
trot. He rode off into the wind, one hand holding
on tight to his big hat. Billy and Splinter dodged
newspaper tumbleweeds blowing across the trail.
A cougar darted across their path and disappeared
down a small canyon. Dust swirled up in little
cyclones, making Billy squint.

Rounding a corner, Billy saw a crowd of towns-people gathered by a small wagon train. A wheel had come off one of the wagons, and the rest were stuck behind it. Men were shouting and yelling at the driver trying to change the wheel. The sheriff ran between the wagons and began guiding the others around the broken one. Weaving through the crowd of townspeople, Billy and Splinter slipped past the wagons.

As they drew near the end of the wagon train, Billy heard a familiar whistle. It was Old Enos, the chuck-wagon cook and maker of great hot dogs, smiling and whistling a crazy tune. Billy waved and rode over to his wagon.

"How are you, Billy Boy?" Old Enos called.

"Fine," Billy smiled. "I'm on a mail run to 44th Street."

"Are you taking the long way or risking the shortcut?"

"We're taking the shortcut, but we'll go real fast! You should relax here for a while, though. There's a wheel off a wagon ahead and you might have trouble getting through."

"Well, Pardner, thanks for the tip." Old Enos grinned and handed Billy a hot dog, with ketchup and mustard creeping over the bun, just the way Billy liked it. "You have a good day now, and be careful."

"Thanks, I will." Billy ate the last bite of bun, jumped onto Splinter, and with Old Enos's whistle fading in the distance, he rode toward the trees.

Slowing as they crossed a small arroyo, Billy and Splinter approached the park. This was the boundary of the Badlands. The roughest part of the mail run lay ahead. Packs of coyotes and a gang of faster, bigger, bandit riders lurked in the shadows. Billy and Splinter started across the park at a gallop, winding around tall cactus, splashing through streams, and slipping down the shadowy trail.

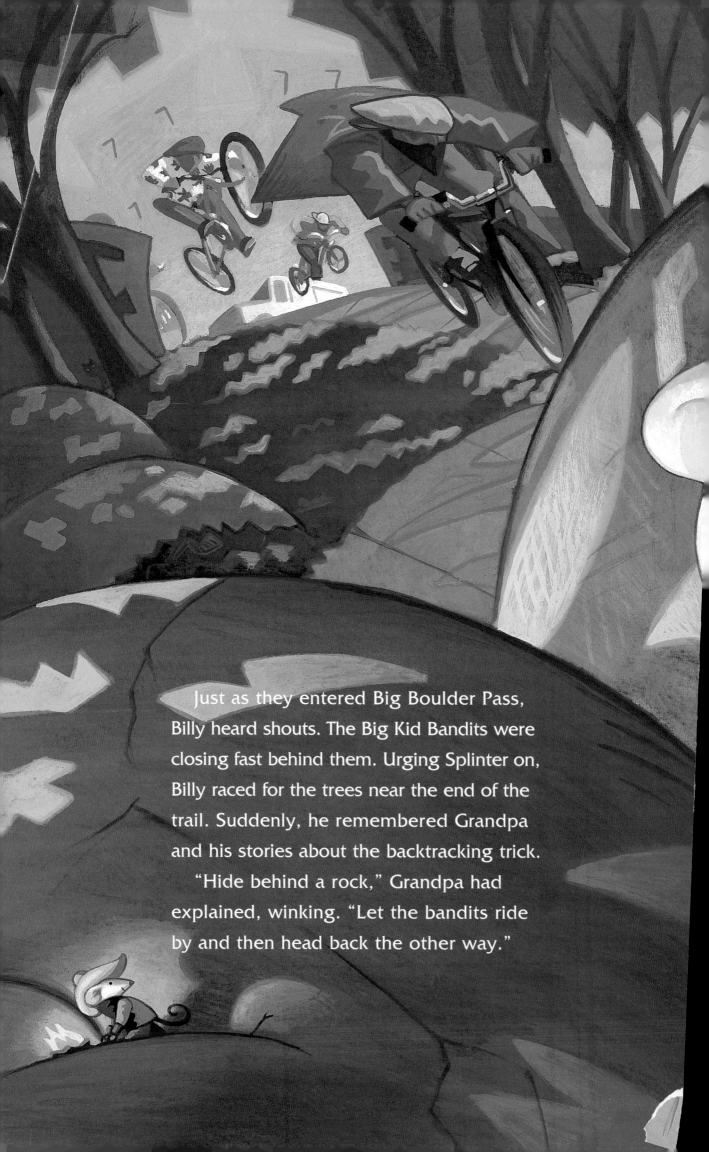

Just as they entered Big Boulder Pass, Billy heard shouts. The Big Kid Bandits were closing fast behind them. Urging Splinter on, Billy raced for the trees near the end of the trail. Suddenly, he remembered Grandpa and his stories about the backtracking trick.

"Hide behind a rock," Grandpa had explained, winking. "Let the bandits ride by and then head back the other way."

Billy leaned over Splinter, and they galloped into the trees. He stopped behind a large rock wall. Billy and Splinter waited quietly, hardly breathing, and listened for the riders.

Whoosh! Whoosh! Whoosh! Whoosh! They raced past, shouting and searching the trail ahead.

Billy grinned as he rode back the way he had come.

Looping around on another park trail,
Billy arrived at the back of the post office.
After emptying his mail pouch, Billy and
Splinter headed for home, taking a trail
that skirted the Badlands.

It was getting dark as Billy tied up Splinter and headed for the bunkhouse. Mr. Higgins met Billy at the front door.

"Did you have a good ride, Billy?" Mr. Higgins asked as they took the elevator up. "Any trouble?"

"Just some bandits, but we gave them the slip."

"You're a good cowboy," Mr. Higgins said. "Here's your floor."

"Would you take me to the top, please? There's someone I want to visit."

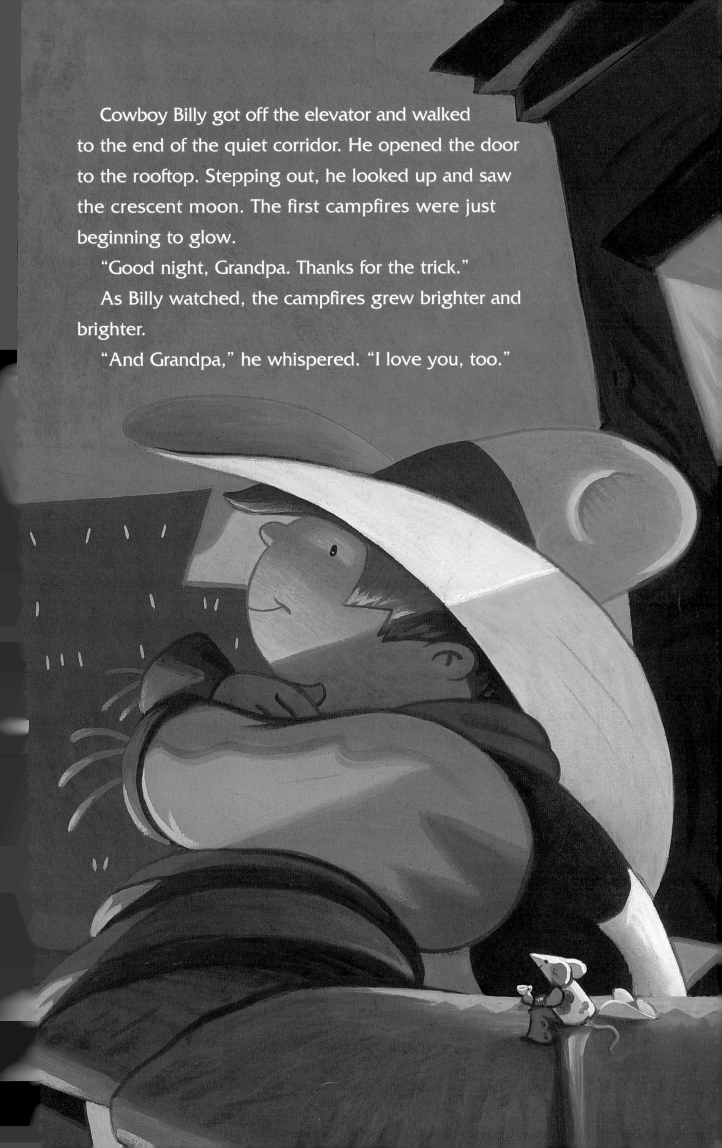

Cowboy Billy got off the elevator and walked
to the end of the quiet corridor. He opened the door
to the rooftop. Stepping out, he looked up and saw
the crescent moon. The first campfires were just
beginning to glow.

"Good night, Grandpa. Thanks for the trick."

As Billy watched, the campfires grew brighter and
brighter.

"And Grandpa," he whispered. "I love you, too."

A NOTE FROM THE AUTHOR

This book grew out of a story I wrote to help my daughters, nieces, and nephews deal with my Dad's death. The story has two important concepts. First, I hope the stars, as a connection between a departed loved one and a child, will help children be comforted and able to cope with such a loss. Second, I hope I reinforce the importance of imagination to both children and adults.

Although we lived in the East, my father loved the West. He filled us with stories about the West and shared his excitement for its culture. He stretched our imaginations and I hope *A Campfire for Cowboy Billy* will do the same for everyone who reads it.

WENDY K. ULMER
grew up in Mt. Gretna,
Pennsylvania, and now
lives in an old farmhouse
near the coast of Maine
with her two daughters,
Amanda and Molly, two
cats, and a dog. She has
been published in
Ladybug and has con-
tributed to a teacher
resource book. She is
a high-school music
teacher, church organist,
and a registered music
therapist. *A Campfire for
Cowboy Billy* is her first
children's book.

KENNETH J. SPENGLER
was born in New York
City and raised in the
suburbs of Philadelphia.
He now lives in
Sacramento, California,
with his wife, Margaret,
and son, Matthew. His
career as an illustrator
began shortly after he
graduated from Tyler
School of Art (Temple
University's art school)
with a B.F.A. His work
can be found on any-
thing from posters to
billboards, and mystery-
book covers to children's
books, including *How
Jackrabbit Got His Very
Long Ears,* also from
Northland Publishing.